D0071483

"*A Possum's Pirate Tale and His Pieces of Eight*, which is brilliantly crafted by Jamey M. Long, is a riveting adventure that is filled with intrigue, emotion, and suspense. The masterful imagery which forces the characters to deal with both sad and happy moments coveys real emotion and an honesty that turns this heartwarming adventure into so much more than just a story. Opie and the little boy are faced with challenges like never before, but their unwavering bravery and their love of family engages the imagination while presenting a powerful message that nourishes the soul. Jamey teaches us through Opie's impeccable character that honor, truth, bravery, respect, and integrity are far more valuable than any buried treasure no matter how many pieces of eight lie within. Readers of all ages will richly be rewarded for joining Opie on his inspiring journey."

-Melissa D. Reedy
The Free Lance-Star

A Possum's

PIRATE TALE

& HIS PIECES OF EIGHT

A Possum's

PIRATE TALE

& HIS PIECES OF EIGHT

written by

Jamey M. Long

TATE PUBLISHING & *Enterprises*

A Possum's Pirate Tale and His Pieces of Eight
Copyright © 2008 by Jamey M. Long. All rights reserved.

This title is also available as a Tate Out Loud product. Visit www.tatepublishing.com for more information.

No part of this publication may be reproduced, stored in a retrieval system or transmitted in any way by any means, electronic, mechanical, photocopy, recording or otherwise without the prior permission of the author except as provided by USA copyright law.

This is a work of fiction. Names, descriptions, entities, and incidents included in the story are products of the author's imagination. Any resemblance to actual persons, events, and entities is entirely coincidental.

The opinions expressed by the author are not necessarily those of Tate Publishing, LLC.

Published by Tate Publishing & Enterprises, LLC
127 E. Trade Center Terrace | Mustang, Oklahoma 73064 USA
1.888.361.9473 | www.tatepublishing.com

Tate Publishing is committed to excellence in the publishing industry. The company reflects the philosophy established by the founders, based on Psalm 68:11,
"The Lord gave the word and great was the company of those who published it."

Book design copyright © 2008 by Tate Publishing, LLC. All rights reserved.
Cover & interior design by Lindsay B. Behrens
Illustration by Brandon Wood

Published in the United States of America

ISBN: 978-1-60696-685-3
1. Youth and Children's Fiction (Ages 6–10)   2. Pirates, Animals, Values, Possums
08.12.08

Yo Ho Ho…a possum's pirate life for me.

On the edge of a small northern town there was a forest. The year was 1657, and a possum was waking up to a bright moonlit night in Great Britain. The possum's name was Opie. Opie was hanging by his tail from a large tree branch high above the ground. As he was hanging upside down, he stretched out his arms, then his legs, and let out a great big yawn. As Opie sat up on his favorite tree branch, he thought about what a beautiful night it was. *I wonder what I should do tonight,* thought Opie. *It feels like a good night to go on an adventure. The only question is where shall I go?*

As Opie walked through the deep green forest, he thought about the boy and his home. He always had fond memories of visiting the

boy and enjoyed the adventures that they had shared. Opie had made up his mind, and he was soon off to see the boy. Opie travelled all night through the quiet forest listening to the sounds of the other animals along the way. As he arrived at the boy's home, the sun had risen high in the sky and was shining down through the tree tops. Opie stepped to the edge of the forest where he could see the boy helping his mother and father with the chores.

Opie quietly sneaked his way across the boy's backyard. When he reached the porch, he saw some people coming down the dirt road that led to the boy's home. The people walking down the dirt road were dressed in fancy uniforms and looked very important. *I wonder who they are,* Opie thought to himself. *Whoever they are, they do not look friendly!*

Opie was right. They were not friendly.

As they approached the boy's home, the boy and his parents warmly greeted them. "Welcome," said the boy's father to the men. "How can we help you?"

"Silence," said the men in royal uniforms. "We are here by decree of the new Lord Protector Oliver Cromwell, and you are under arrest for treason."

Treason, thought Opie. *That is ridiculous. The boy and his family would never do anything to betray their country.*

"We are not guilty of treason," desperately replied the boy's father. "We are loyal to England." However, it was no use. The royal guards put them all in shackles and began to take the boy and his family away.

"Where are you taking us?" yelled the boy. "This is a mistake!"

The guards laughed. "By order of Lord Cromwell, we are sending you to Barbados

where you will spend the rest of your lives working as slaves," the royal guards replied. The royal guards continued marching the boy and his family away from their home. Opie was a smart possum and had heard about Lord Protector Oliver Cromwell before. He knew he was not a nice man and had accused many people of doing things when they were really innocent. Many people had lost their homes and their lives because of him. Opie knew in his heart that the boy and his family were innocent. "This is very bad," said Opie. "The boy is my friend, and I must try to help him." Opie did not think twice. He quickly took off down the dirt road. He followed the boy and his family with his fur flying in the wind, being careful to stay out of sight along the way.

After a long journey, the boy and his family were taken to a dock where they were boarded onto a large wooden ship. They were still surrounded by the royal guards. "I must get on that ship," exclaimed Opie. He turned his head to see if anyone was around. When he decided that it was safe, he quickly scurried up the side of the ship and onto the deck. After he had made his way onto the main deck, he could see the boy and his family being taken to the decks below. Opie again scurried behind the boy and his family before the royal guards closed the hatch to the bottom decks locking them below. The boy and his family could not see anything, but Opie was able to find them without a problem. As a possum he was able to see things very clearly in the dark. Opie moved close to the boy to make sure that he was okay and to keep him company. A few minutes later, Opie could feel the ship start to move. Opie crawled back up on to the main deck to see what was going on. Once he was there, he saw that the ship had left its port. They were now on their way to Barbados.

After a long voyage, the ship that was carrying the boy, his family, and Opie arrived in Barbados. Once the ship docked in the port, the boy and his family were taken off the ship and were soon sold to work for a master. Their master was a very cruel and mean man. He treated the boy and his family horribly. Opie felt sad for the boy and his family. *I wish there was something I could do to help them*, thought Opie sadly.

Just then, Opie saw the boy's father whispering to another man. It was very hard for anyone else to hear what they were saying but not for Opie. Opie was glad that he did not have a problem hearing anything since he had big ears and could hear almost any sound.

"Do you see that man over there?" said the father to his son.

"Yes," replied the boy. "You mean the man with the torn pants digging a hole?"

"Yes, that is the one," replied the boy's father. "Now listen to me very carefully. He is going to escape tonight, and he has agreed to take you with him. I want you to listen to what he says. He will get you out of here and to freedom. His name is Greaves."

"Are you and mother coming to?" asked the boy.

"No, son," replied the boy's father. "We cannot escape with you."

"Then I do not want to go," replied the boy with tears in his eyes. "I do not want to leave you."

"You must," said the father sternly.

The boy understood what his father was trying to do and finally agreed to go. "I will

escape," the boy said to his father. "But I promise I will come back one day and rescue everyone."The boy hugged his dad as the man digging the hole motioned for him to leave. As Opie overheard the entire conversation, he realized that the boy would need him. *I better go with the boy in case he needs me,* said Opie to himself. He quickly scurried off after the boy and the strange new man that was only known as Greaves.

The boy and Greaves ran as fast as they could across the island, and Opie was not far behind. They finally crossed the entire island until they came to the Carlisle Bay. There were several ships docked there. "What do we do now?" the boy asked Greaves.

"We need to sneak onto one of those ships and get off this island," Greaves said to the boy.

Which ship do we sneak up on? Opie

wondered as he looked at all of the wooden ships with their big bellowing sails. Greaves looked around at all of the ships at the dock. He saw one at the end of the bay that was getting ready to sail. "That one," exclaimed Greaves. "Let's go."

Greaves, the boy, and Opie quickly ran after the ship that was now in the water. "We will never catch it," said the boy.

"Yes we will," replied a determined Greaves. "Now swim as though your life depended on it."

The boy and Opie quickly realized that it did. They jumped into the water and swam until they were alongside the ship. "Now how do we get on board?" the boy asked Greaves.

Greaves and the boy looked around and saw a rope from one of the main sails hanging down. "Climb the rope," Greaves yelled to the boy.

Opie watched as the boy climbed the rope until he was safely aboard. Opie then grabbed hold of the rope and also pulled himself on board. They were all standing on the main deck of the ship and were looking around. The boy saw a man standing with his back to him wearing fancy clothes. He was also carrying a parrot on his right shoulder. "That must be the captain," whispered the boy, since he heard him giving orders to the other crewmembers. The man was dressed in a bright red coat with gold embroidery, wearing brown leather boots with buckles. The man was also wearing a white puffy shirt, a bright sash around his waist, and a three-cornered hat with a feather on top of his head. As the man walked down the deck, the boy could also see that he wore an eye patch over his left eye and carried a long sword. As the man turned around, Opie and the boy were able to get a better look at him.

Opie was a very curious possum, and he wanted a better look at this strange figure. He began climbing up the main mast that held the ship's sails. He climbed and climbed until he was high above the ship and could see everything that was going on. As Opie looked at the captain, he began to get worried. The captain did not look like a nice sea captain at all. He looked mean.

"That must be the captain," whispered the boy to Greaves.

"That is no ordinary captain," said Greaves. "That is a pirate captain and no ordinary pirate captain either. That is Captain John Hawkins!"

Opie had never seen a pirate captain before and did not know what one was. *I sure hope we will be able to get to safety on this ship,*

Opie thought to himself. "Who is Captain John Hawkins?" the boy asked Greaves.

"He is one of the cruelest pirate captains that have ever lived. He is feared by everyone. We must not let him see us. The boy and Greaves began looking for a place to hide. Luckily, no one had seen them sneak on deck so no one knew they were there. Or so they thought. Someone was quickly approaching. Before Opie could climb back down the mast to warn them, the ship's Master snuck up behind Greaves and the boy and grabbed them.

"Captain," said the ship's Master. "Look what we have here, stowaways!"

Captain Hawkins walked over to them. "Stowaways you say," replied the captain.

"Aye," said the ship's Master. "What shall we do with them? Should we let them go?"

Captain Hawkins and the crew laughed,

and for a moment Opie thought that everything would be okay. But he soon realized it was not. The captain quickly lost his smile, and his face turned serious. "No one sneaks on my ship and just leaves," said Captain Hawkins harshly to Greaves and the boy. "You will sign the ship's articles and become a part of my crew. You will pillage and plunder all of the ships and islands that we come across."

Greaves was forced to sign the ship's articles and to become a member of the crew, but the boy still refused. "I will not become a pirate!" sternly replied the boy.

"You are a brave lad," laughed Captain Hawkins. "You do not have to become a pirate. Instead I will keep you as a prisoner down in the decks below. You will never see daylight again!"

"This is horrible," exclaimed Opie. "There

has to be a way to help the boy. But before Opie could do anything, the ship's Master was taking the boy down below the decks.

As the days passed, Opie was still sitting on top of the mast hiding in the large sails. He was trying to figure out a way to rescue the boy. Opie looked down and saw that the pirates were eating, throwing food, singing, and carrying on. "I bet the boy is hungry," said Opie. "I will go down there, grab him some food, and take it to him."

Opie bravely hurriedly scurried down the mast until he was back on the main deck of the ship. When none of the pirates were watching, he made his way under the table where they were all eating. Opie found a piece of cloth and began putting the scraps of food into it. Once he had enough, he tied the ends to his tail and scampered toward the hatch that led to the decks below. Opie lifted the deck hatch and climbed below without being seen. He found the boy sitting in the corner with a dimly lit candle that provided the only light below deck. Opie untied the cloth with the food in it and left it for the boy. The boy was very hungry and ate all of the food, but could not see Opie in the dark.

Opie felt good knowing he was able to help the boy. After the boy ate all of the food, he noticed that something was drawn on the piece of cloth. It appeared to be a drawing of an island named Tortuga with a big *X* on it. "What is this?" said the boy as Opie leaned in for a closer look. The boy picked it up and realized that the piece of cloth was indeed a genuine treasure map.

Hidden treasure, thought Opie. *If we ever get out of this mess, I bet we could find it and share it with everyone.*

Below deck Opie and the boy could hear

quite a bit of commotion on the main deck. "What is going on up there?" said the boy. "I sure hope my friend Greaves is okay."

Opie decided that he had better go back up on the main deck to see what was going on. On deck, Opie did not want to be seen so he looked for a good place to hide. He spotted a large black cannon on the side of the ship. Next to the cannon were a pile of cannonballs that made an excellent place for a curious little possum to hide and to see everything that was happening. On the main deck, Greaves was becoming a very proficient pirate. He was an honest and moral man. He had already earned the respect of his fellow crewmen. Greaves was nothing like Captain Hawkins, and the entire crew knew that.

Greaves was becoming so popular with the crew that they decided they no longer wanted to sail under Captain Hawkins' command. Greaves knew what a horrible captain Hawkins really was, and he wanted to help the crew. He knew what had to be done. He must challenge Captain Hawkins and lead a mutiny with the crew against him.

Neither Greaves nor the crew was aware that Captain Hawkins was close by and could hear their plan to mutiny against him. Captain Hawkins drew his long sword and walked over to Greaves, challenging him to a duel. The crew was still very scared of the captain, and they all ran away. Greaves held his ground and did not move.

Opie looked and saw that Greaves did not have a sword to fight Captain Hawkins. He looked around and saw a sword lying close by the pile of cannonballs he was hiding behind. Opie could not reach the sword with his paw, but he could reach it with his tail. He quickly

grabbed the sword with his tail and flung it through the air. Greaves saw the sword flying through the air and grabbed it before Captain Hawkins struck him with his sword.

The duel went on for quite a while up and down the main deck. Opie and the crew watched on. Greaves and Captain Hawkins made their way to the plank at the back of the ship. Greaves finally had Captain Hawkins cornered and asked him to surrender. "Never!" shouted Captain Hawkins. Just then, the plank snapped, and Captain Hawkins fell into the ocean down to Davey Jones' Locker.

The crew was now free from the terrible Captain Hawkins. They all cheered for Greaves and voted to make him their new captain. "What is your first order of business?" the ship's Master asked Greaves.

"To free the boy," replied Greaves. Opie could not contain his excitement, and he yelled for joy. Greaves went below deck, with Opie close behind, and released the boy. When the boy learned that Greaves was the new captain of the ship, he handed him the treasure map.

"What is this?" Greaves asked the boy.

"It appears to be a treasure map," eagerly replied the boy.

"Aye, it does indeed," replied Greaves.

"Do you think we can find it?" the boy asked Greaves.

"I suppose we can," replied Greaves. "Let's see if the crew agrees."

"Aye, Aye," happily shouted the crew.

"It is settled then," said Greaves. "We are off to Tortuga to find the buried treasure."

Opie was excited. He loved to go on new adventures, and now he had a chance to find buried treasure. He knew this would be a fun adventure and was ready to go. As the

sun was setting, the crew set sail and began heading for the island of Tortuga.

"How will we know when we are at Tortuga," the boy asked Greaves. Opie was also wondering this. To him, all islands looked the same.

"Tortuga is easy to find," laughed Greaves. "It is the only island that is shaped like a turtle. It is even called 'Turtle Island.'"

That is my kind of place, thought Opie. He liked the sound of an island being named after a fellow animal. The boy looked over the bow of the ship and could see a large island with a unique shape appearing in the distance. It looked like a turtle. "Land Ho," exclaimed the boy.

"Land Ho," also exclaimed an excited Opie, who was also peeking over the bow of the ship. The ship slid out of the ocean and onto the sandy beach. The boy, Opie, and

Greaves climbed down a rope on to the island. The boy pulled out the treasure map and saw that it led one hundred paces into the jungle. The jungle looked like Opie's home, and he could not contain his excitement. He quickly took off running making sure to count off his hundred paces along the way. The boy and Greaves were not far behind. At the end of the one hundred paces, they came to a large rock. On the rock were some small Spanish coins.

"What are those?" asked the boy.

"Those are pieces of eight," replied Greaves. "Pieces of eight are coins that can be spent all over the world." The boy checked the map as Opie waited anxiously for the next clue.

"According to the map, we are supposed to walk two hundred paces to the east," said the boy. Opie, the boy, and Greaves continued

walking through the dense jungle until they reach two hundred paces. They came to another large rock with more pieces of eight on it. Opie looked around wondering where the treasure was. The boy checked the map again. "From here," continued the boy, we must go fifty paces to the north and then X marks the spot."

Everyone was excited. They quickly walked fifty paces, with Opie far in the lead. When they came to the end of the fifty paces, they did not see any treasure. "Where is the treasure?" asked the boy. "It is supposed to be right here."

Opie looked around and saw that there were two logs lying on top of each other making an X pattern. He quickly began digging with his paws. Sand was flying everywhere. Before long, he had dug a huge hole. As Opie was getting tired, he scooped out some more sand with his paw and heard a "thunk." Opie had found the treasure chest. He pulled the chest out with his long pink tail just in time for the boy to find. "The treasure is over here," exclaimed the boy.

Opie was smiling to himself as he hid behind some big plants resting from all of that digging. "Congratulations," said Greaves to the boy. "You have found the treasure, and it is all yours. What are you going to do with all of it?"

The boy looked at all of the treasure and thought for a moment. "I am going to share it with everyone," said the boy. "There is enough here to free my family and the other people being kept unjustly on Barbados. There is also plenty left over for you and your crew to enjoy." There was even enough treasure left over for Opie to enjoy for himself.

"You are a very generous young boy," said Greaves kindly.

Opie was very happy to hear this. He knew the boy was a good person and would do the right thing with the treasure. Before the boy closed the lid to the treasure chest to take it back to the ship, Opie climbed inside until he was safe on board. The boy and Greaves made their way back to the ship and set sail toward Barbados to free the boy's family. Once they arrived, the boy was able to free his family, along with the other people on the island, with the treasure he had found. Captain Greaves, who had now earned the nickname Red Legs since his pants were short and his legs were burned from the sun, sailed them all back home on his ship.

Once back at England, it was time for the boy, his family, and Opie to say goodbye to Captain Greaves. Before they parted, captain Greaves gave the boy the treasure chest with the remainder of the treasure.

"Will I ever see you again?" the boy asked Greaves.

"If you are ever in the Caribbean you can find me there," replied Greaves. "I will be spending the rest of my days on my plantation trying to do good deeds for those around me."

"I wish you luck and will miss you," replied the boy as he waved goodbye.

Opie poked his head from out of the treasure chest just in time to see Captain Greaves sail away on his ship into the sunset. The boy and his family began to head for their home. Opie climbed out of the treasure chest and was eager to get back to his home in the forest as well. Opie walked close behind the boy and his family, making sure that they returned home safely. Once he knew they were safe, he began walking back through the forest singing "Yo Ho Ho" and sharing his pieces of eight with the other animals in the forest.

listen|imagine|view|experience

AUDIO BOOK DOWNLOAD
INCLUDED WITH THIS BOOK!

In your hands you hold a complete digital entertainment package. Besides purchasing the paper version of this book, this book includes a free download of the audio version of this book. Simply use the code listed below when visiting our website. Once downloaded to your computer, you can listen to the book through your computer's speakers, burn it to an audio CD or save the file to your portable music device (such as Apple's popular iPod) and listen on the go!

How to get your free audio book digital download:

1. Visit www.tatepublishing.com and click on the e|LIVE logo on the home page.
2. Enter the following coupon code:
   1131-2a33-705f-4d06-9a8d-4f6b-c4bc-4ace
3. Download the audio book from your e|LIVE digital locker and begin enjoying your new digital entertainment package today!